The Missing Mummy

SCHOLASTIC

ACTION™

Welcome to This Book

Have you ever thought about being a detective? Imagine being the one to solve a crime and save the day.

In this story, Dink, Josh, and Ruth Rose have a chance to do just that. They're at a museum looking at mummies. Then something strange happens. A woman steals a child mummy right before their eyes. They chase her. But she disappears. Later, the mummy's tomb is robbed of its treasure. So Dink, Josh, and Ruth Rose start searching for clues.

Will they solve the mystery? What surprises will they find along the way?

Target Words

These words will help you understand the mystery of the missing mummy.

- **amateur:** someone who is new at something; not an expert

  Dink, Josh, and Ruth Rose are amateurs, but they may be able to solve the case.

- **exhibit:** a public show or display

  The mummy exhibit has turned into a crime scene.

- **intruder:** a person who enters a place without permission

  The intruders must have known where the mummy's treasure was kept.

Reader Tips

Here's how to get the most out of this book.

- **Map** Look at the maps at the front of the book. Look at the compass in the lower right-hand corner. What do you think N, E, S, and W stand for?

- **Plot** The plot is the series of events that take place in a story. They give it a beginning, middle, and end. The plot also includes the characters and setting. In this story, three friends are at a museum when something happens. As you read, try to keep in mind the events that unfold.

This one is for Mitchell Sanders, with love.
—R.R.

To my Mummy and Daddy.
—J.S.G.

Text copyright © 2001 by Ron Roy.
Illustrations copyright © 2001 by John Steven Gurney.
All rights reserved. Published by Scholastic Inc., 557 Broadway, New York, NY 10012, by arrangement with Random House Children's Books, a division of Random House, Inc.
Printed in the U.S.A.

ISBN 0-439-58895-2

SCHOLASTIC, SCHOLASTIC ACTION, and associated logos and designs are trademarks and/or registered trademarks of Scholastic Inc.

A TO Z MYSTERIES is a registered trademark and the A to Z Mysteries colophon is a trademark of Random House, Inc.

LEXILE is a registered trademark of MetaMetrics, Inc.

2   3   4   5   6   7   8   9   10   23   12 11 10 09 08 07 06 05 04 03

A to Z Mysteries

The Missing Mummy

by **Ron Roy**

illustrated by
John Steven Gurney

SCHOLASTIC INC.
New York Toronto London Auckland Sydney
Mexico City New Delhi Hong Kong Buenos Aires

Contents

Chapter 1 1

Chapter 2 11

Chapter 3 17

Chapter 4 25

Chapter 5 33

Chapter 6 43

Chapter 7 52

Chapter 8 63

Chapter 9 69

Chapter 10 75

Glossary 84

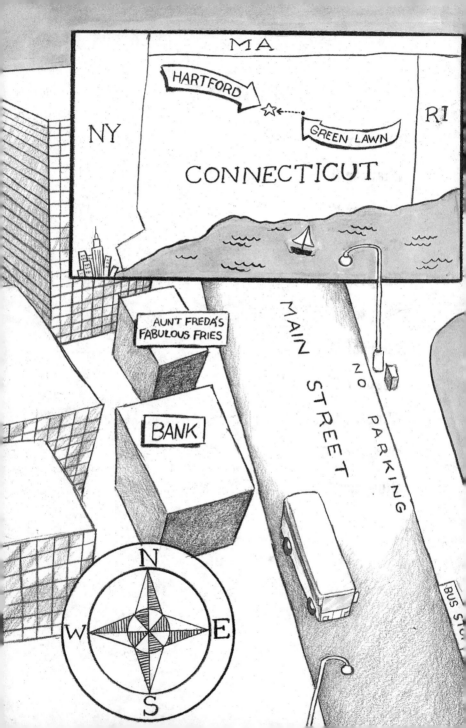

CHAPTER 1

"Mummy Monday at the museum?" Josh said. He peered over Dink's shoulder at the Sunday newspaper. "So what's the next day, Tummy Tuesday?"

It was summer vacation, and Dink, Josh, and Ruth Rose were lying on the lawn behind Dink's house. Josh's dog, Pal, was snoozing under a tree.

Ruth Rose took the paper and read the article quickly. "No, Josh, the next day is about dinosaurs," she said. "It's called Tyrannosaurus Tuesday."

"The museum is having programs for kids all week," Dink explained.

"So what happens on Wednesday?" Josh asked.

"Kids go to the Connecticut River and study plant and animal life," Ruth Rose said. "It's called Wet Wednesday."

Dink took the newspaper back from Ruth Rose. "And the next day, you get to make a horror movie—that's Thrilling Thursday. The last day is Frog Friday. Each kid gets to study a frog."

"So let's sign up!" Josh said. "How much does it cost?"

Dink scanned the page. "A dollar for each program," he said. He looked at Josh and Ruth Rose. "That's five dollars for all five days."

"I don't have five bucks," Ruth Rose said.

"Me neither," said Josh. "But I know how we can earn it."

"How?" Dink asked.

"My dad's been trying to get the barn cleaned out," he said. "I bet he'd give us the money if we did it for him."

"Great idea!" Dink said.

The kids ran to Josh's house and spent the rest of Sunday working. Brian and Bradley, Josh's two little brothers, helped by playing with Pal.

Josh's dad gave each of the kids seven dollars for their hard work.

After lunch the next day, Dink, Josh, and Ruth Rose got on a bus to Hartford. Fifteen minutes later, the bus dropped them off on Main Street, in front of the Wadsworth Museum.

Across the street was a bank. A digital sign over the bank's entrance said MONDAY, JULY 10, 82 DEGREES. Then the sign flashed the time: It was nearly two o'clock!

"Come on, guys," Dink said. "We only have a few minutes to sign up."

They ran up the museum's front steps and through the wide doors. Inside, the museum was air-conditioned and quiet. The floor was made of marble. Tapestries and large paintings covered the white walls.

"Welcome to Mummy Monday," said a woman standing behind a counter.

Across the lobby, a bunch of other kids and a few grownups were already waiting. Ruth Rose took a map from a rack just inside the door. Then the kids walked over to join the group.

They each gave the woman behind the counter a dollar.

"I wonder where they keep the mummies," Josh whispered.

At exactly two o'clock, a door behind the counter opened and a tall man walked out. He was wearing a tan jacket and shorts, knee socks, laced boots, and a white helmet.

"I'm Dr. Harris Tweed," the man said. "Today, I will take you on a journey to ancient Egypt."

Dr. Tweed's face, hands, and knees were deeply tanned. Dink wondered how much time he had spent in the Egyptian desert.

"Who's ready to follow me into a tomb?" Dr. Tweed asked. He smiled, showing big white teeth that made his tanned face even darker.

"We're going in a *tomb*?" Josh muttered. "I think I want my dollar back!"

"Shh," Dink whispered.

Dr. Tweed's eyes narrowed. "If you're afraid of mummies, now's the time to speak up."

"Ugh!" a girl with red hair said. "Won't the mummies smell?"

"Today, you will learn precisely why mummies *don't* smell," said Dr. Tweed. "Now please, follow me to the tomb!"

They walked to an arch at the rear of the lobby. Through the arch was a room with rows of benches facing a blank stone wall. The wall was built of large, flat rocks fitted closely together. Dink wondered how the museum people got those huge rocks inside.

"The tomb—and the mummies—are on the other side of this wall," Dr. Tweed said. "Before we go inside, I want to tell you a little about how these people died, and how they became mummies."

He pointed to the benches. "Please be seated."

"Let's sit in front," Dink said, heading for a bench.

When everyone was seated, Dr. Tweed began speaking in a deep voice. "Close your eyes and imagine you are standing on the bank of the River Nile four thousand years ago. Feel the sun on your back. See the river as it flows by. Hear the oxen bellow as they labor in the fields."

A hush fell over the group.

"Suddenly, an earthquake shakes the ground!" Dr. Tweed shouted.

Dink's eyes popped open as goose bumps crept up his arms. All the kids opened their eyes and stared at Dr. Tweed.

"Later," he continued, "the survivors prepare the dead for burial. Three of the people who died in that earthquake are with us today."

Dr. Tweed walked over to the wall and pressed his hand against one of the stones. Immediately, the wall slid open.

Through the opening, Dink could see a dim room. The stone floor was partly covered with sand and gravel.

"What you see is the burial tomb," Dr. Tweed said quietly. "Come in, please, but speak only in whispers and touch nothing."

"This is so great!" Ruth Rose whispered as they entered the tomb.

The tomb was cold, and Dink shivered. Old pots and farming tools were scattered around the floor. Strange-looking symbols were painted on the walls.

Off to one side were three stone coffins.

CHAPTER 2

One of the coffins was lying on a stone table. The other two were leaning upright against the walls to either side. Dink noticed that the coffin on the table was smaller than the other two.

"You are standing in an actual Egyptian tomb," Dr. Tweed said in a hushed voice. "It was brought here in pieces and then reconstructed."

He pointed at the coffins. "An ancient Egyptian coffin is called a *sarcophagus.* Each sarcophagus holds a mummy. In a moment, I will open the lids. But first, take a moment to appreciate the fine artwork."

On each lid, jewels and gold had been used to create a mask. *The faces look peaceful, almost happy,* thought Dink.

"The Egyptians believed that people who died would need their money in the next life," Dr. Tweed said. "So rich people were often buried near their wealth."

He pointed through an arch into another room. "That is the treasure chamber," he said. "You'll get a chance to look in there after we view the mummies."

Ruth Rose raised her hand. "How come one of the coffins is so small?" she asked.

Dr. Tweed walked over to the sarcophagus on the table. "This sarcophagus contains a child mummy," he explained. "The little boy died with his parents, who now stand beside him for eternity."

Dr. Tweed placed his hand on a standing sarcophagus. "This is the boy's mother," he said. Using both hands, he swung the lid open.

"And the father." Dr. Tweed opened the other standing sarcophagus.

Without saying another word, he removed the lid of the smallest sarcophagus and leaned it against the wall.

The kids stared at the three mummies. Each was covered with some kind of cloth, yellowed with age. Dink realized that Dr. Tweed was right—there was no smell at all.

"Each mummy is wrapped in strips of linen," Dr. Tweed said. "Beneath the cloth—"

Suddenly, a woman with long blond hair who was wearing a baggy dress darted forward. She snatched the child and raced out of the tomb.

"Stop!" Dr. Tweed shouted, bolting after the woman.

Everyone in the room began talking at once. Before the kids could figure out what to do, Dr. Tweed hurried back into the tomb. "Quiet, please," he said. "Um, it seems Mummy Monday will have to be postponed. We'll have it tomorrow."

"But tomorrow is Tyrannosaurus Tuesday!" someone said.

Dr. Tweed looked flustered. His tanned face had turned pale, and one of his eyelids was twitching. "Yes, of course, you're right," he said. "I'll schedule another mummy day for next week. Now you'll have to leave the tomb. I'm very sorry."

Kids mumbled, "No fair" as they

filed out. Dr. Tweed stepped aside to let them pass.

"Why would anyone steal a mummy?" Josh asked as he, Dink, and Ruth Rose followed the other kids.

"I read somewhere that gold and jewels were wrapped up with the bodies," Ruth Rose said. "Maybe that mummy has valuable stuff inside the cloth."

"You mean that woman is gonna unwrap the mummy?" Josh asked. "Gross!"

Dink, Josh, and Ruth Rose were the last kids out of the tomb. A moment later, Dr. Tweed hurried past. Behind them, the tomb door closed with a rumble.

"This is so bogus," Josh said. "Should we just go home?"

"I have to use the rest room first," Ruth Rose said.

The kids found the rest rooms

around the corner from the tomb. The door to the ladies' room opened, and a smartly dressed woman with short dark hair stepped out. She was carrying a briefcase and talking on a cell phone.

"We'll wait for you here," Dink said as Ruth Rose slipped into the rest room.

"I wonder what the thief did with the mummy," Josh said. "I mean, she couldn't exactly carry it down Main Street!"

Suddenly, the rest room door crashed open. Ruth Rose stood there looking as if she'd seen a ghost.

"Ruth Rose, what's the matter?" Dink said.

"G-get Dr. Tweed," she answered. "It's in the rest room!"

"What's in the rest room?" Josh asked.

Ruth Rose took a deep breath. "The missing mummy!" she said.

CHAPTER 3

Dr. Tweed was standing by the front doors talking with two police officers. Dink dashed over to them. "Excuse me," he said, his mouth suddenly dry.

"Can we help you?" one of the officers asked. The name tag on her shirt read S. WASHINGTON.

"My friend found the mummy in the ladies' room!" Dink said.

"Show us," said the other officer. His name tag read P. PETERS.

Everyone rushed over to where Josh and Ruth Rose were standing outside the rest rooms.

"Will you come inside with me?" Officer Washington asked Ruth Rose.

Ruth Rose and the officer walked into the rest room. A few seconds later, they both came out again.

"Dr. Tweed, will you step in with me, please?" Officer Washington said.

Dr. Tweed followed the officer back inside the rest room.

"So where was it?" Josh asked Ruth
Rose.

"You know those tables they have so
parents can change a baby's diaper?"
she said. "It was right there on the
table!"

"In plain sight?" Dink asked.

Ruth Rose nodded. "At first I
thought it was a big doll, so I took a
closer look. . . ."

"Yuck!" Josh said.

The rest room door opened again. Officer Washington walked out, with Dr. Tweed behind her. He was carrying the child mummy in his arms.

"The mummy seems to be undamaged," Dr. Tweed said. "But I'll have to examine it in my office."

Dr. Tweed and the two police officers crossed the lobby and disappeared through the door behind the counter.

"I guess we might as well go home," Dink said.

"Some Mummy Monday," Ruth Rose grumbled.

"Look, there's a cafeteria," Josh said. "Let's get something to drink."

The kids entered the large room, paid for cold drinks, and sat at a round table.

"I wonder where the thief went after she left the mummy in the rest room," Ruth Rose said as she sipped her lemonade.

"What do you mean?" Dink asked.

"There weren't any windows in there, so she couldn't have gotten out that way," Ruth Rose said. "And if she'd come through the door, she would have bumped right into us."

"But a woman did come out," Josh said. "Remember, she was talking on a cell phone?"

"Yeah, but she looked totally different," Ruth Rose said.

"Maybe she was in disguise," Dink said. "Maybe the mummy snatcher changed clothes in the rest room!"

"She might've hidden her dress in the briefcase," Josh said. "And the blond hair could've been a wig."

"Guys, I just realized something," Ruth Rose said. "When that woman came out of the rest room, she walked toward the tomb. Maybe she went back to steal something else!"

The kids left their drinks on the table and ran to the tomb.

"Open, sez me!" Josh said. He pressed the stone and the door rumbled open.

Tiny lights shone from the tomb ceiling, casting shadows on the floor.

The child mummy's sarcophagus lay empty. Its lid still leaned against the wall. The other two mummies stood guard over the room.

Ruth Rose grabbed Dink and Josh and pointed them toward the treasure chamber. Without speaking, the three tiptoed under the arch.

The treasure chamber, like the tomb, had a stone floor partly covered with sand and gravel. The walls were also stone, with no windows.

"She's not here," Dink whispered,

glancing into the chamber's dim corners. His arms suddenly bristled with goose bumps.

"Yeah, but look at all the gold!" Josh said, pressing his nose up against a glass display case.

There were six cases in the

chamber. Four were filled with pottery and farming equipment. The other two held gold carvings and jewelry.

"You'd think if someone wanted to steal something," Dink said, "it'd be this treasure, not a mummy."

"These cases are locked, and they have alarms," Ruth Rose said. She pointed to thin gray wires running along the edges of each case.

Suddenly, Dink heard a low rumbling noise. "What's that?" he asked.

"It sounds like the tomb door!" Ruth Rose said.

The kids ran back into the tomb. They were just in time to see the wall slide shut.

Josh ran to the wall and tried to force it open with his fingers. When he turned around, his face was white.

"We're locked in!" he said.

CHAPTER 4

"There must be a way to open the door from in here," Ruth Rose said. "Let's look for a switch or something."

The kids searched the walls near the door but found nothing that would open it.

"But why did the door close in the first place?" Josh asked.

"You might have set off an alarm when you touched the case," Ruth Rose said.

"If she's right," Dink said, "someone will hear the alarm and come to see who's in here. All we have to do is wait."

"Wait in here?" Josh squeaked.

"It won't be for long," Dink said. "Any second now, that door will slide open again."

"Yeah, well, let's wait in the treasure chamber," Josh muttered. "Those mummies are creeping me out."

"They're just dust," Ruth Rose said.

"But they're *dead* dust!" Josh said, heading into the chamber.

The kids sat on the floor and leaned against a wall. The room was silent. The ceiling lights cast a soft glow onto the gold inside the cases.

"I've always dreamed of being locked in a room full of gold," Josh said. "But now that I am, I'd rather be home."

Minutes passed, then more minutes. No one came to rescue them. The stone door in the tomb remained solidly shut.

"No one knows we're in here," Josh muttered. "We could be trapped forever. We'll die and become mummies!"

"Our parents all know we're at the museum," Ruth Rose said. "If I'm not home for supper, my dad will call."

"But by then the museum will be closed," Josh insisted. "No one will answer the phone!"

"Then my folks will drive here," Ruth Rose said.

"Or they'll call the police," Dink said. "All we have to do is sit here and chill out."

"I'm *already* chilled," Josh mumbled. "This place feels like the inside of a refrigerator."

Dink grinned. "Gee, Joshua, I

thought you'd be happy inside a refrigerator."

"Very funny, Donald!" Josh muttered. "Plus, I'm sitting on gravel. Why can't they have carpets like normal people?"

Ruth Rose stood up and wiped gravel and sand off her shorts. "Josh is right. Let's see if we can find someplace more comfortable to sit," she said.

"Like home," Josh said.

"Or like this!" Ruth Rose said. She had opened a small door cut into the stone wall.

"It's some kind of closet," Dink said, peering inside.

"Egyptians didn't have closets," Josh said. The kids saw folding chairs, cleaning supplies, and a stack of carpet pieces.

"The carpet squares must be for kids to sit on," Ruth Rose said. "Let's spread them out."

The kids covered the closet floor with carpet squares, then lay down.

"This is more like it," Josh said, making himself comfortable. "Now if someone would just bring me some pizza and a soda, I'd be happy."

"Would you share it with the mummies?" Ruth Rose asked Josh.

"Nope."

More time passed. Dink yawned, and his eyes grew heavy. He pulled the closet door shut, darkening the small room. Then he lay down, and they all drifted off to sleep.

Suddenly, a huge blast shook the room. The folding chairs fell over with a crash, and a box of cleaning stuff flew off a shelf.

Dink, Josh, and Ruth Rose bolted up out of a sound sleep.

"What the heck was that?" Josh said. "It sounded like a bomb!"

"I smell smoke!" Ruth Rose said in the dark.

Dink opened the closet door a crack, then pulled it shut again. "The place is filled with dust," he said, wiping his eyes.

"What happened?" Ruth Rose asked.

Just then Dink heard voices.

"Someone's out there," Josh said. "We're rescued!"

"Quiet!" Dink whispered. "They wouldn't bomb the place to rescue us."

Dink nudged the door open a crack. He peered through the floating dust, then suddenly scooted back.

Two shapes in dark clothing slipped past the closet, inches from the kids' noses. Both carried black gym bags.

As the kids watched, the two figures separated, stopping in front of two of the glass cases. Dink heard glass breaking, and then a piercing alarm bell sounded.

"Grab as much as you can. Then we're outta here!" one of the intruders said.

"They're not here to rescue us," Dink whispered. "They're here to steal the mummies' gold!"

CHAPTER 5

The thieves worked fast. Through the door crack, Dink watched the two dark forms fill their satchels with the gold.

"Jeez, this stuff is heavy," one of them grunted. The crooks dragged the heavy satchels across the floor.

Dink tried to memorize the black clothing, the thieves' ski masks, and the satchels. As the crooks passed the closet, he noticed that one of them seemed to have a white stripe between his waist and knees.

Then both were gone, and the treasure chamber was quiet.

Dink waited several seconds, then pushed the closet door all the way open.

The gold was gone. Two large hunks of stone lay on top of broken glass. Dust covered everything.

As Dink, Josh, and Ruth Rose stepped out of the closet, the alarm bell stopped as suddenly as it had started.

"Where did they go?" Josh whispered in the now silent room.

Before Dink could answer, they heard the tomb door slide open. A second later, Officers Peters and Washington stormed into the treasure chamber.

"Freeze!" Officer Peters shouted. Then he took a second look. "What . . . it's the kids!"

Dr. Tweed appeared behind the two

officers. "Please explain why you're in here," he said. One of Dr. Tweed's eyes was twitching.

"We were trying to find the woman who took the mummy," Ruth Rose said. "Then the door closed all by itself."

"We fell asleep in the closet," Josh said. "A few minutes ago, we heard a loud bang. Then two guys came in and stole the gold!"

Dr. Tweed stepped over broken glass and examined the shattered cases. "Nothing is left," he said. "A priceless treasure has been stolen."

"Let's check out the wall," Officer Peters said.

Everyone followed him into the tomb. A large, jagged hole had been blown through one of the walls. Through it, Dink could see the tall, thick shrubbery behind the museum.

The floor around the hole was

littered with chunks of stone, but the
two standing mummies didn't look
damaged. On the table, the child
mummy's coffin was closed. The mask
on its lid stared peacefully up at the
ceiling.

"Well, thank goodness!" someone shouted. Dink turned around. His parents ran into the tomb.

Ruth Rose's parents came in next, quickly followed by Josh's folks.

"What happened to you kids?"

Dink's mom asked, giving him a hug. "We've been calling practically the whole city of Hartford for hours!"

"We got locked in," Josh said. "We were trying to find the mummy snatcher!"

"What mummy?" Ruth Rose's mom asked.

"Let's save the story till we get home," Dink's dad suggested. "You kids must be starving."

"I am!" Josh said.

At ten the next morning, Officers Peters and Washington stopped by Dink's house. Dink called Josh and Ruth Rose, and they all sat in the backyard.

"I hope you got a good night's sleep," Officer Peters said, smiling. "We just talked to your parents, and they said it would be okay if we asked you some questions."

"If that's okay with you," Officer Washington said.

The kids nodded.

Officer Peters glanced at his notes. "We think the woman who stole the mummy wanted to get everyone to leave the tomb," he explained. "In all the confusion, someone hid a small bomb near the wall."

"We've had a chat with Dr. Tweed," Officer Washington added. "Now we'd like to hear your part of the story."

The kids explained everything that had happened up until they had been awakened by the bomb blast.

"Sometimes," Officer Washington said, "in the excitement of the moment, we forget small things. I'd like you to think back to the point when you saw the two thieves enter the treasure chamber. Tell me everything you remember, even the smallest detail."

Dink went first. "Well, they were both wearing dark clothes. I think they had ski masks over their faces."

"One of them talked," Ruth Rose said. "He said—"

"It was a man's voice?" interrupted Officer Peters.

Ruth Rose closed her eyes for a minute. "I think so. It was a low voice," she said. "He said, 'Let's grab as much as we can and get out of here.'"

"Did the other one say anything?" asked Officer Washington.

Ruth Rose thought for a minute. "I think one of them said whatever they were carrying was heavy," she added.

Officer Peters nodded and made a note.

"I remember smelling something," Josh said.

Both officers looked at him.

"I don't know what it was, but . . ."

Josh stopped, looking embarrassed.

"We're listening," said Officer Washington. "You smelled . . ."

"It was something to eat, I think."

Officer Peters smiled at Josh.

"What, hamburgers, pizza . . . ?"

Josh shook his head. "Sorry, I can't remember."

"I remember something else!" Dink said suddenly. "One of the guys had a white stripe on his clothes."

"A white stripe?" Officer Peters repeated. "I thought they were dressed in dark clothes."

Dink nodded. "They were, but I saw a white stripe right here."

He stood up and drew an imaginary line just above his knees.

"Did you see him from the front or back?" Officer Washington asked.

"Both," Dink said. "But the stripe was just in front."

The officers took notes, then closed their pads.

"You've been very helpful, kids," Officer Washington said. She looked at Josh. "If you remember that smell, give me a call." She handed him a card.

Josh took the card. "Um, can we go back to the museum?" he asked. "Today is Tyrannosaurus Tuesday!"

"Sure," Officer Washington said. "Just be careful of those big teeth!"

CHAPTER 6

At one-thirty that afternoon, the bus dropped the kids off in front of the museum. The digital sign over the bank said 90 DEGREES.

"We've still got a half hour," Josh said. "I could use a snack."

"Josh, we just ate!" Ruth Rose said. "I think you're part wolf."

Josh growled and wiggled his eyebrows.

"It's too hot to eat, anyway," Dink

said. "Let's go sit in the shade for a few minutes."

The kids followed a gravel path around the side of the museum. They passed trees, shrubs, and flower beds. At the corner of the building, they found a goldfish pond and a few benches. Fat goldfish came to the surface, as if expecting food.

"Look!" Josh said, pointing at the back wall of the museum. "That must be where the bomb blew up."

A large sheet of plywood covered the blasted-out hole. Bags of cement and a stack of cinder blocks stood nearby.

"The crooks must have run right past this bench," Josh said.

The kids sat down. From their bench, they could see the bank clock on Main Street.

"I wonder where they went," Dink said. "They couldn't have carried that gold far."

Ruth Rose pulled the museum map from her back pocket. On one side was a drawing of the rooms inside the museum. On the other side was a map showing the little park, the museum, and Main Street.

Josh pointed at Main Street. "Maybe they had a getaway car waiting," he said.

Ruth Rose shook her head. "Parking isn't allowed in front of the museum. If the crooks had left a car there, the police would have noticed it."

"And there are no other streets near the museum where they could have parked," Dink observed, studying the map.

Josh glanced around at the trees and shrubs. "So where did they take the gold?" He looked down at the ground. "Maybe they buried it!"

Dink shook his head. "They were in a hurry. I can't see them taking the time to dig a hole," he said. He checked the digital sign in front of the bank. "Anyway, we'd better get inside. It's almost two o'clock."

The kids left, following the path back around to the front of the museum.

"Yum, I smell something good," Josh said as they hurried up the front steps.

"You're *always* smelling something good," Ruth Rose said.

They entered and paid the woman behind the counter. An inflated rubber tyrannosaur stood in the center of the lobby. In its teeth, it held a sign that said FOLLOW THE ARROWS.

A minute later, the kids found Dr. Tweed standing outside an open door.

"Hello again," he said. "Come on in. We're just about to start."

A bunch of kids were sitting in a circle of desks. Dink, Josh, and Ruth Rose slid into three empty seats. In the middle of the circle stood a giant dinosaur skeleton. Its huge head almost touched the ceiling!

"I'm sure most of you recognize *Tyrannosaurus rex*," Dr. Tweed said.

Dink stared up at the skeleton. He tried to picture what the massive dinosaur would have looked like when it was alive.

"Today," Dr. Tweed went on, "we are going to study this prehistoric carnivore—"

A boy in the front row raised his

hand. "Did you get the mummy back?" he asked.

"Yes, one of our guests found it in the ladies' room," Dr. Tweed said. "Now, as I was say—"

"I saw on TV that someone broke in and stole the treasure," a girl said.

Dr. Tweed sighed. "Yes, that is true. The thieves are still at large, and the treasure is missing. But we are here to discuss dinosaurs today."

He opened a cupboard and pulled out a long bone. "A tyrannosaur leg fossil," he said. "This dinosaur lived and died in what we now know as Utah. You can touch the bone, but please be gentle."

The kids crowded around Dr. Tweed to touch the fossil.

"What do we know about the tyrannosaur?" Dr. Tweed asked.

Answers came swiftly:

"They had big teeth!"

"They ate other dinosaurs!"

"They laid eggs!"

"Good," Dr. Tweed said. "Did you also know that *Tyrannosaurus rex* had an amazing sense of smell? It could smell its food from hundreds of yards away."

"Like Josh," Dink whispered.

"And *T. rex* also had a very small brain for his size," Dr. Tweed went on.

"Like Dink," Josh mumbled.

Dr. Tweed dimmed the lights and showed slides. The kids learned how the dinosaur lived, what it ate, and how it raised its young.

When the slide show was over, Dr. Tweed turned the lights up again. He pulled open a cupboard. "Now you can construct your *own* dinosaur." He asked for volunteers to pass out clay, wood, and wire.

"Your creation will stand on the wood. Use the wire to help shape the legs and tail."

Soon twenty pairs of hands were building miniature tyrannosaurs.

"This is fun," Josh said. "Maybe I'll be a sculptor instead of a painter."

Ruth Rose looked at Josh's pile of clay. "Josh," she said, "we're supposed to make dinosaurs. Yours looks like a potato."

"Very funny," Josh said. Then his eyes opened wide. "That's it!"

"That's what?" Ruth Rose asked.

"That's what I smelled last night when we were in the closet!"

"Potatoes?" Dink asked.

Josh shook his head. He closed his eyes and sniffed. "French fries!" he said.

CHAPTER 7

Dink shaped a tail for his dinosaur. "All I smelled was dust from the bomb. How could you smell French fries?"

Josh was making a row of teeth for his tyrannosaurs. "Because I have an amazing sense of smell," he said.

"I'm afraid we've run out of time," Dr. Tweed said. "You may take extra clay and finish your sculptures at home."

He handed out cardboard boxes for carrying the clay dinosaurs.

"Thank you all for coming," Dr. Tweed said as everyone got up to go. "Tomorrow is Wet Wednesday. I will be away, but one of my colleagues will be here in my place. Be sure to wear shorts and old sneakers, and bring permission slips from your parents."

A few minutes later, Dink, Josh, and Ruth Rose stood in front of the museum holding their boxes.

"What time does our bus come?" Josh asked.

"They run every half hour," Ruth Rose said, glancing across the street at the bank clock. "It's three-thirty now. We must have just missed one."

Josh grinned. "Good, we have time to get a snack."

Dink rolled his eyes. "Josh, my folks are still freaked about the bomb. I promised I'd get right home after the museum today. Let's just go wait in the shade."

They walked around to the little pond and sat on a bench. Immediately, the goldfish came up for handouts.

Suddenly, Josh stood up and stuck his nose in the air. "I smell it again!" he said. He swiveled his head, like a periscope looking for enemy ships.

"There!" he said, pointing back along the park path toward Main Street. A small restaurant stood next to the bank.

A sign in the window said AUNT FREDA'S FABULOUS FRIES.

"Forget your stomach, Josh," Dink said. "The next bus will be here soon."

Josh slumped back on the bench.

"I'm being falsely accused," he said. "All I'm trying to do is figure out what happened to that gold."

"Okay," Dink said. "So tell us."

"Okay," Josh said. "I smelled French fries last night. They sell French fries across the street. So maybe the robbers work there. Maybe *that's* where they took the gold!"

"I saw those crooks dragging the gold," Dink said. "There's no way they carried it all the way to that restaurant."

Ruth Rose looked at Dink. "Still, Josh might be right about the thieves working there," she said. "Maybe we should go over and check it out."

"But our bus . . ."

"Come on, Dinkus," Josh said, standing up. "We'll catch the next one."

"Okay, but I still think it's just a trick," Dink said. "You'd do anything for a plate of fries."

The kids carried their boxes through the park, across Main Street, and into the restaurant.

They sat in a booth by the window. Overhead, a ceiling fan hummed, and a jukebox played an Elvis song.

Six teenagers were just leaving. They left behind a small mountain of dirty dishes and glasses.

A roly-poly woman came through a swinging door with three glasses of ice water. She had gray hair and wore a white apron over her dress.

"Welcome to Aunt Freda's," she said. "I'm Aunt Freda. I'll bet you've been to the museum, right?"

"How did you know?" asked Ruth Rose.

The woman pointed to Ruth Rose's

small box. WADSWORTH MUSEUM was printed on the side.

"We made dinosaurs out of clay," Josh said.

"Oh, that would be Dr. Tweed," Aunt Freda said. "He's one of my regular customers. So, what can I get you today?"

"Fries and a lemonade, please," said Josh.

"You'll love my fries," Aunt Freda said. "The best in Hartford!"

"I'll have the same," Ruth Rose said.

Dink made it three, and Aunt Freda bustled away to the kitchen.

Josh leaned forward and whispered, "Maybe Aunt Freda was one of the robbers!"

Dink grinned. "She doesn't exactly look like a robber," he said.

"Plus, the crooks were taller and thinner," Ruth Rose said.

Aunt Freda returned with their fries, drinks, ketchup, and napkins. "Let me know how you like my fries," she said. "It's my secret recipe!"

The kids dug in, sharing the ketchup.

A few minutes later, a woman with short dark hair came out of the kitchen. She was wearing an apron and carrying a large plastic tub.

The woman walked over to the table with the dirty dishes and began cleaning up. Dink heard her grunt as she lugged the loaded dish container into the kitchen.

"What's the matter?" Ruth Rose asked Dink, who was staring after the departing woman.

Josh waved a French fry in front of Dink's face. "Why the big eyes, Dink?"

"That woman," he said. "The way she was lugging that pile of dishes . . . she reminded me of one of the robbers last night."

"Hot diggety," Josh said. "At last someone agrees with me!"

Ruth Rose turned and looked toward the kitchen. "You know, she has short dark hair just like the woman who came out of the rest room before I found the mummy."

The three kids stared at the kitchen door.

"And she smells like French fries!" Josh said.

CHAPTER 8

Aunt Freda walked over to their booth. "My, you did a good job on those fries," she said. "Anything else?"

"No, thank—" Dink started to say.

"Yes!" Ruth Rose interrupted. "Could you show us how you make your fabulous fries? Donald here is really interested in cooking."

I am? thought Dink.

Aunt Freda beamed at Dink. "Of course, dearie. Come on back to the kitchen," she said.

Ruth Rose nudged Dink, and they all followed Aunt Freda.

On the other side of the swinging door, the smell of frying potatoes hung heavy in the air.

A row of wall shelves held pots and pans, cooking spices, cookbooks, and a bunch of bottles and jars. Against one wall stood a pile of crates bulging with raw potatoes.

The woman with short dark hair was standing at a counter, slicing potatoes. She was wearing earphones and didn't seem to notice the kids.

Dink stared at the woman. As she stooped over a pile of potatoes, Dink imagined her stooped over a case of Egyptian gold.

Aunt Freda interrupted his thoughts. "Come over here," she said, leading the kids to a deep-fry machine.

She lowered her voice. "Here's my

secret. I put a little garlic and vinegar right in the olive oil," she said, then winked. "Promise you won't tell?"

Dink nodded. "Promise," he said. "Boy, cooking potatoes is *really* interesting!"

From the corner of his eye, Dink saw Josh scoop something off the kitchen floor and shove it in his pocket.

Then Ruth Rose poked Dink. She pointed her chin at a coatrack by the back door. A black jacket hung from one of the pegs. On the floor sat a black gym bag.

"Anything else you want to know?" Aunt Freda asked.

"No, thanks," Ruth Rose said, smiling. "We've seen everything we need."

The kids left the kitchen, with Aunt Freda following them. They paid for their food and started for the door.

Suddenly, Aunt Freda put her hand on Dink's arm. "Wait!" she said, digging into the pocket of her apron. "Put out your hands!"

The kids obeyed, and she dropped a candy into each palm. "Have a nice day," Aunt Freda said, then opened the door for them.

The kids popped the candies into their mouths as they hurried back to their bus stop.

"Did you see that jacket?" Ruth Rose said. "If that woman put it on over her apron, the white edge would show. Is *that* what you saw last night, Dink?"

"It could be," Dink said. "And that gym bag looked like the ones the robbers were carrying."

Josh shook his head. "You guys are such amateurs," he said. "The jacket could belong to anyone, and there are a million black gym bags in Hartford."

He reached into his pocket. "But I found a *real* clue!"

He held out a smooth pebble the size of an M&M.

"What's that?" Dink asked.

"Come on, I'll show you." Josh headed for the museum steps.

Dink and Ruth Rose followed Josh through the lobby. In front of the tomb, they found a sign announcing that the mummy exhibit was closed. Behind the sign, the sliding door was shut.

Josh walked over to the wall and pressed the stone. With a rumble, the wall slid open.

Josh leaned inside and scooped a handful of the gravel off the floor. Then he closed the door again.

"See, they're the same," Josh said, holding up the gravel and the pebble he'd found at Aunt Freda's.

"I don't get it," Dink said.

"I found this pebble on the floor in Aunt Freda's kitchen," Josh explained. "It matches the pebbles in the tomb. The only way it could have gotten from the tomb floor to Aunt Freda's floor was on the bottom of one of the crook's shoes!"

"Okay," Ruth Rose said. "But that still doesn't tell us where the gold is."

"Or who the second crook is," Dink added.

"Maybe not," Josh said, "but *something* in that restaurant smells!"

CHAPTER 9

That night, a thunderstorm blew through Green Lawn. While Dink slept, lightning flashed and thunder boomed outside his bedroom window.

Dink had a nightmare. He was trapped in the tomb again. This time he was alone.

One by one, the two mummies leaning against the wall opened their eyes. One by one, they stepped out of their coffins and shuffled toward him.

They passed the child's coffin. Its lid stayed shut, the child's mask staring up at the ceiling.

Because the mummy's not in there, Dink thought. *But then why—*

Just then Dink felt a cold hand on his shoulder. He tried to run, but his legs wouldn't budge. The mummies' cloth wrappings had come loose and were encircling his body, like tentacles.

Dink bolted awake with a yell, tangled in his sheet. When he realized that he was in his bed and not the tomb, he lay back down.

He tried to go back to sleep, but something kept him awake. It was something in his nightmare, in the tomb. What was it?

He lay there trying to picture the tomb again. Before the bomb went off, all three sarcophagus lids had been open. The small sarcophagus was empty because the mummy was still in Dr. Tweed's office.

But after the blast, the smallest coffin—the one for the child—was closed.

Then Dink remembered the robbers dragging those two heavy bags of gold. He smiled, closed his eyes, and went back to sleep.

After breakfast, Dink called Josh. He came over, and they walked next door to Ruth Rose's house. She was sitting on her front steps with a plate of toast on her knees.

Dink sat on the bottom step. "I figured it out last night," he told them. "I know where the crooks hid the gold."

Josh reached for a piece of Ruth Rose's toast, but she slapped his hand.

"Don't you know it's nice to share?" he asked.

"Don't you know it's nice to ask first?" Ruth Rose said. But she passed Josh a section of her toast. "Tell us, Dink."

"I had an awful dream last night," Dink said. "I was trapped in the tomb. The two big coffins were open, and the mummies were chasing me. But the little coffin, the one for the kid, was closed."

He looked at Josh and Ruth Rose. "After I woke up, I remembered something. When we were in the tomb just before we got locked in, the little coffin was open. Remember? But when we went back into the tomb after the bomb went off, the coffin lid was closed!"

"I don't get it," Josh said, licking jam from his fingers.

"You will in a minute," Dink said. "I couldn't get back to sleep last night, so

I started wondering: Who closed that little coffin? Then it hit me. If the robbers didn't have a car waiting, and if the gold was too heavy to carry far, maybe they hid it *there!*"

"Then the crook has to be someone who can get back into the tomb later and get the gold," Josh said.

"DR. TWEED!" Ruth Rose yelled.

"That's what I think, too," Dink said. "Aunt Freda said Dr. Tweed was a good customer. I figure he and the woman with the short dark hair planned it together."

"She had that gym bag," Ruth Rose said. "And all she had to do was walk across the street."

"And she smelled like a walking French fry!" Josh added.

"But which one hid the bomb?" Ruth Rose asked.

"Dr. Tweed, I think," Dink said.

"Remember how he stayed in the tomb for a few minutes after we all left?"

"But why did the woman grab the mummy?" asked Josh.

"To get us out of there," Dink said. "Dr. Tweed had to be alone in the tomb so he could plant the bomb."

Dink grinned at Josh and Ruth Rose. "And that left the sarcophagus empty for the gold!" he said.

"OH MY GOSH!" Ruth Rose yelled. "Dr. Tweed told us he wouldn't be at Wet Wednesday today. I'll bet he's gonna take the gold and leave!"

She jumped up and ran into the house. Dink and Josh were right behind her.

Ruth Rose called the police station and asked for Officer Fallon.

CHAPTER 10

Officer Fallon drove Dink, Josh, and Ruth Rose to Hartford.

He had called Officers Peters and Washington. The two cruisers met down the street from the museum.

"Officer Washington will nab the young woman in the restaurant," Officer Peters told Officer Fallon. "You and I will take the museum. Kids, you come with us."

Dink, Josh, and Ruth Rose—flanked

by the two officers—crossed Main Street and entered the quiet museum. They followed the hallway until they came to Dr. Tweed's office door.

With the kids standing behind him, Officer Peters knocked. When there was no answer, he turned the knob and opened the door. "Not here," he said.

Officer Fallon and the kids peered into the office. They saw the little mummy lying on a table.

Officer Peters looked at Dink, Josh, and Ruth Rose. "Let's check that tomb," he said.

DR. TWEED

The kids and the two officers walked back through the lobby. They stopped in front of the closed tomb door.

"How do we get in?" Officer Fallon asked.

"I know!" said Josh. He pressed the secret stone, and the door slid open. Dr. Tweed was standing in front of the small sarcophagus.

He whipped around, clasping a lumpy gym bag to his chest. In the sarcophagus, Dink saw a pile of gold objects.

Dr. Tweed's eyes were blinking and twitching at the same time.

"Hello there," Officer Fallon said. "Taking a trip?"

Dr. Tweed lunged toward the plywood-covered hole in the wall. Swinging both hands, he smashed the gym bag into the wood. The wood crunched and fell outward, and Dr. Tweed leaped through the opening.

Outside, he tripped over a bag of cement and plunged into the goldfish pond. The gym bag sank to the bottom.

Dr. Tweed flopped around in the shallow pond, then sat up, spitting out water. Lily pads hung from his ears and slimy algae dripped from his eyebrows.

"I need to call my lawyer," he sputtered.

Just then Officer Washington walked into the park. She was leading the woman from the restaurant, who wore handcuffs.

"So she talked?" Officer Peters asked his partner.

"Yep. These two were supposed to take a taxi to the airport in a few minutes," Officer Washington said. "Their next stop was Europe, where they hoped to sell the treasures."

"Take her away," Officer Peters said. "I'll bring our wet friend along in a few minutes."

Officer Washington led her prisoner out of the park.

Officer Peters stepped into the pond and helped Dr. Tweed to his feet. He leaned the wet thief against a tree and snapped handcuffs onto his dripping wrists.

Officer Fallon pulled off his shoes and socks and waded into the pond. He lugged out the gym bag, filled with Egyptian treasure and pond water.

"Thanks for your help," Officer Peters told Officer Fallon. "I'll call you later."

Officer Peters picked up the heavy gym bag with a grunt. He nudged Dr. Tweed forward, and the two left the park. Their sopping shoes made squishing noises as they walked.

Officer Fallon sat on a bench next to Dink, Josh, and Ruth Rose. He wrung pond water from his dripping pant legs.

"Good job, kids," he told them.

Then he pulled out his pad, opened to a fresh page, and began writing. He paused.

"In all the excitement," Officer Fallon said, "I've forgotten what day this is."

The kids grinned at each other.

"It's Wet Wednesday!" Josh told him.

Glossary

accuse *(verb)* to say that someone has done something wrong (p. 56)

amateur *(noun)* someone who is new at something; not an expert (p. 66)

ancient *(adjective)* very old (p. 5)

beam *(verb)* to smile (p. 63)

burial *(noun)* the placing of a dead body in a grave (p. 8)

chamber *(noun)* a large room (p. 12)

coffin *(noun)* a box into which a dead body is placed (p. 9)

disguise *(noun)* an outfit that hides a person's real identity (p. 21)

eternity *(noun)* forever (p.13)

exhibit *(noun)* a public show or display (p. 67)

fossil *(noun)* the remains of an animal or plant that have been preserved in rock (p. 49)

intruder *(noun)* a person who enters a place without permission (p. 31)

labor *(verb)* to work (p. 7)

massive *(adjective)* very large (p. 48)

postpone *(verb)* to put off until later (p. 14)

precisely *(adverb)* exactly (p. 6)

satchel *(noun)* a bag (p. 33)

shrubbery *(noun)* bushes (p. 35)

tapestry *(noun)* a piece of cloth with pictures or patterns woven into it (p. 4)

tomb *(noun)* a grave, room, or building for holding a dead body (p. 6)

About the Author

Ron Roy is the author of more than thirty-five books for children, including *A Thousand Pails of Water, Where's Buddy?,* and the award-winning *Whose Hat Is That?* When he's not writing a new story for the A to Z Mysteries® series, Ron spends time traveling all over the country, and restoring his old Connecticut farmhouse.